Absolutely Speechless

Stephanie slid into her desk not thirty seconds before the late bell rang! Although Kate and I sit right behind her, she didn't turn around to whisper anything to us.

At lunchtime Stephanie bolted out and raced to the cafeteria. But Kate, Patti, and I were close behind.

"Now we can talk," I said to Stephanie. "So come on. . . . What was your dad's big surprise?"

"Well . . ." Stephanie said. "I had no idea where Dad wanted to take me, right?" She paused. Stephanie usually loves surprises, but she didn't seem to be enjoying this one very much.

"Stephanie! Was yesterday fabulous or what?" someone screeched practically in her ear.

It was the dreaded Jenny Carlin!

"Kevin was even better-looking than he is on TV, didn't you think?" Jenny shrieked even louder.

"Better-looking than he is on TV!" Kate said in a stern voice. "That was your surprise? You saw Kevin DeSpain *in person*, Stephanie?!"

Patti and I stared at Stephanie, absolutely speechless.

Look for these and other books
in the Sleepover Friends Series:

SLEEPOVER FRIENDS

Starstruck Stephanie

Susan Saunders

AN
APPLE
PAPERBACK

SCHOLASTIC INC.
New York Toronto London Auckland Sydney

ISBN 0-590-42817-9

12 11 10 9 8 7 6 5 4 3 2 1   0 1 2 3 4 5/9

Printed in the U.S.A.

First Scholastic printing, February 1990

Chapter
1

"If you're extra-nice to me, maybe I'll introduce you to Kevin DeSpain . . . ," a screechy voice echoed across the Riverhurst Elementary School cafeteria.

"I couldn't bring myself to be *extra-nice* to Jenny Carlin if she were the last person on earth!" Stephanie Green muttered.

"Robin Becker and Tracy Osner don't seem to be having any trouble," Patti Jenkins said. Robin's in our class, and Tracy's in 5A. They don't usually hang out with Jenny Carlin, but today both of them were hovering around her in the middle of the lunch line.

Kate Beekman made a face. "Some people have no self-control!" she said.

I was thinking to myself that I'd do almost any-

1

thing to meet Kevin DeSpain. I'm Lauren Hunter, and Kevin's just about my favorite actor of all time. But Jenny Carlin and I are sworn enemies, ever since Pete Stone, whom she liked at the beginning of the year, decided he liked me instead. Of course he dumped me after about five minutes and got interested in Kathy Simon and then in Barbara Paulsen. But I'm the one Jenny's still mad at!

"Kevin DeSpain's actually coming to Riverhurst, and who gets to meet him? Jenny Carlin! Sometimes I think there's no justice in the world!" Patti said as she set a plate of carrot sticks down on her tray with a thump. She, Stephanie, Kate, and I were at the front of the lunch line, filling our trays with the usual Monday cafeteria fare: carrot sticks, steamed vegetables, a bagel with melted Swiss cheese.

"Come on, guys. Cheer up!" Stephanie said. "We're riding our bikes out to Chesterfield this afternoon, and we'll get to see Kevin just like Jenny Carlin."

"From a distance, *maybe*. But you know they won't let us anywhere near him," I said, staring gloomily at the bowl of limp squash one of the cafeteria ladies had handed me. "My favorite movie star in the whole world comes to my own hometown, and he might as well be on the moon!"

2

"Then he'd be an astronaut, which would make him a lot more interesting," Kate said with a grin. "Anyway, if you want to see Kevin, all you have to do is turn on your — "

"I know, I know!" I interrupted crossly. "Turn on your television sets on Tuesday!" Kate's attitude about Kevin really annoyed me. Just because she didn't happen to think Kevin DeSpain was the best actor in the universe, so what. He's the dreamiest!

Kevin's on *Made for Each Other* every Tuesday night at eight on Channel 12. He's the gorgeous guy with dark, wavy hair and big green eyes who plays the private detective with bionic powers. Marcy Monroe plays his partner. In the show they travel all over the place in Kevin's antique biplane, investigating crimes. They've been to San Francisco, a country inn in Vermont, New York City, a ranch in Texas . . . and now *Riverhurst*!

Or, at least, Chesterfield. Chesterfield's this huge old estate four miles up the Pequontic River. It used to belong to a very rich man, and now it belongs to the Riverhurst Association for the Preservation of Historic Homes. On the estate there's a three-story brick mansion built like an English manor house, greenhouses full of rare plants, a giant fish pond, and an enormous lawn that slopes down to the river. And a two-hour episode of *Made for Each Other* was going to be shot there that week! I still couldn't believe it!

"If we'd known about it sooner, of course, we could have worked out a brilliant plan," Stephanie murmured, reaching for her bagel. "Like disguising ourselves as Chesterfield gardeners!" Stephanie's great at plans, and this one didn't sound bad to me. Chesterfield has the most famous gardens in the state, and a whole troop of gardeners working practically around the clock to keep them looking good.

"We're a little young to be professional gardeners, don't you think?" Kate asked. "Besides, movie producers always keep the shoot's location a secret for as long as possible. It holds the crowds down." Kate would like to be a director some day, so she knows about these things.

"Well, it's not fair!" I said. I grabbed my full tray and stalked across the cafeteria to our regular table. "Just because Jenny Carlin's father happens to be on the Preservation Council . . ."

"That's an idea. Kate," Stephanie burst out excitedly, "maybe your dad could volunteer his services as their doctor for the week. Then we could come along as his assistants!"

Kate sighed. "Give me a break, Stephanie! You practically faint when you get a paper cut. Some assistant *you'd* make. Anyway, my dad has better things to do than sit around waiting for Kevin DeSpain to come down with a case of the sniffles!'' she added huffily. She slid onto a folding chair next to me. "Like save people's lives at the hospital!''

Dr. Beekman is a cardiologist, and heart problems *are* more important than common colds, no matter *who* has the cold. But sometimes Kate can be so superior! Stephanie certainly thought so when she first met her. She said Kate was a total know-it-all! Of course, Kate said Stephanie was an airhead who could only talk about shopping. I guess they were both a teeny bit right, but fortunately each of them has so many good qualities that you'd hardly notice the others. In fact, Kate and I have been best friends practically all our lives with hardly a disagreement.

We both live on Pine Street in Riverhurst. Since we're almost next-door neighbors — there's only one house between us — we started playing together when we were still in diapers. By kindergarten we were best friends for life. That's when the sleepovers started. Every Friday night either I'd spend the night at Kate's, or she'd stay over at my house. It got to be such a regular thing that Dr. Beekman named us the Sleepover Twins.

Not that there's anything very twinlike about

Kate and me. We certainly don't look alike: Kate's short and blonde, I'm tall with dark brown hair. And we don't act, or even *think*, alike, either. Kate's the most sensible person I know, while I tend to let my imagination run away with me. Kate's super-neat; I'm definitely messy. I'm kind of a jock; Kate goes out of her way to avoid sports. She's always organized, and I'm usually not.

Still, I once figured out that Kate and I spent around eight thousand hours together including sleepovers without a single major argument.

That all changed when Stephanie Green moved to the other end of Pine Street from the city last year. I got to know Stephanie because we were both in 4A, Mr. Civello's class. She knew all the latest dances and fashions, and in fourth grade, she already had her own style of dressing, like always wearing clothes that are red, black, and white. She also told terrific stories about her life back in the city.

I thought she was great, and I was sure Kate would, too. So I invited Stephanie to a Friday sleepover at my house, so the two of them could get acquainted.

Talk about your major disaster! On that first night, both of them decided that *one* face-to-face meeting was enough to last them a lifetime! Neither of them ever wanted to spend a single minute to-gether again! But I can be plenty stubborn when I want to. And I was sure they'd get to like each other if they'd only give it a chance. . . .

Since the Greens' house is also on Pine Street, it was only natural that Stephanie ended up biking to school with Kate and me. Then I asked Stephanie to meet me at the mall a couple of Saturdays, when I knew Kate would be there. Once we'd cleared those hurdles without any drastic blow-ups, Stephanie invited me to her house for a sleepover. And I said I'd only do it if Kate came as well.

At that sleepover we ate dozens of Stephanie's mom's fabulous peanut-butter-chocolate-chip cook-ies, which thawed Kate out a little. Then we watched three movies in a row on Stephanie's private TV. That definitely put Kate in a friendlier frame of mind, and finally she broke down and asked Stephanie to a sleepover at her house. Slowly but surely, the Sleep-over Twins became a trio.

Not that Kate and Stephanie were suddenly in total agreement about everything — no way! Which is just one of the reasons I was glad when Patti Jenkins turned up in Mrs. Mead's room this fall, along with the rest of us.

Patti's from the city, too. Compared to Stephanie, though, who's bubbly and outgoing, Patti's really quiet and shy. She's one of the smartest kids in our class, as well as one of the *nicest*. She's also even taller than I am, which I consider a definite plus. Stephanie's as short as Kate, and I was getting kind of tired of being the giant of the group.

Stephanie wanted Patti to be part of our gang. "It would even things out," she said. That wasn't any problem for Kate and me, since we both liked Patti right away. So school had barely started this year and there were *four* Sleepover Friends!

Patti's as crazy about Kevin DeSpain as Stephanie and I are. "It's too bad the movie isn't set in ancient times," she said as she sat down across the table from Kate and me. "My mom could volunteer as an advisor." Both Patti's parents teach history at the university. Mrs. Jenkins specializes in ancient history and Mr. Jenkins in modern. But Patti's dad was away at a conference that week. "But then I guess there wouldn't be any reason for them to be in Chesterfield. They'd be shooting the movie in Greece, or Italy," she went on.

Kate started to giggle. "Can't you just imagine Kevin and Marcy on the banks of the Pequontic, in togas and sunglasses, solving ancient crimes?" Kate said that because Kevin almost always wears sunglasses on the show.

"Very funny," Stephanie said, sitting down beside Patti. "I'm sure Kevin would look *great* in a toga."

Kate laughed, but not for long, because just then Jenny Carlin came walking across the cafeteria toward us. She came to a stop at the table closest to ours, set her tray down and bounced onto a chair. Then she went right on talking without missing a beat.

"Daddy's the one who got them a permit to make the movie, you know," Jenny announced. Tracy, Robin, and Jenny's faithful sidekick, Angela Kemp, hung on her every word. Naturally, Jenny was talking loudly enough to be heard on the other side of the world.

She turned slowly in our direction. Jenny looks a lot like my kitten, Rocky. She has green eyes set wide apart, a button nose, and a pointy chin. I knew she was dying to see what kind of reaction she was getting from the four of us.

"Just ignore her!" Kate hissed. She took a big bite of carrot stick and chewed noisily.

"Who could ignore that voice!" Stephanie muttered under her breath.

"The producer was so grateful that he promised he'd take Mom and Dad and me out to dinner on Friday," Jenny practically shrieked. "With the stars — Marcy and *Kevin*!"

Stephanie almost choked on her bagel. I felt kind of sick myself. Jenny Carlin, having dinner with my favorite actor?! "Patti's right," I mumbled. "There's no justice in the world."

Stephanie glared at Jenny Carlin. Then she scooted her chair around until she had her back to Jenny's table.

She leaned toward me. "Don't worry about it, Lauren," she said, tapping her collar bone. "Jenny Carlin may have connections, but we have our secret weapons."

Chapter 2

Our secret weapons were the four T-shirts we'd had printed the weekend before at Trendy. Trendy is this store on East Main Street that sells a few art supplies, and tons of posters and buttons of rock groups and movie stars. Barry Kline, the owner, stocks lots of sweatshirts and T-shirts, too, and he'll print special ones for you while you wait.

As soon as we'd read in the *Riverhurst Clarion* about the episode of *Made for Each Other* being shot at Chesterfield, Stephanie started thinking of great gimmicks to get Kevin DeSpain to notice us. "We need something special, something that'll make him instantly pick us out of the crowd!" Stephanie said. "The way people in studio audiences wear wild outfits so they'll get chosen for game shows."

"No way I'm going to wear a gorilla suit," Kate said firmly. "Or dress up in purple and green and pretend I'm an eggplant." She raised an eyebrow at Patti and me to show she was joking.

But Stephanie was dead serious when she answered, "No. That probably wouldn't work. I don't know if Kevin *likes* gorillas. Or eggplants. But I read once in *Teen Topics* that he loves girls who wear glasses! Maybe we could buy some of those huge tortoise-shell frames at Toys Galore. . . ."

"I don't ever wear glasses out, not even as a joke," Kate said huffily. She's a little nearsighted, but she refuses to put on her glasses unless she's watching a movie in a theater.

"Wait. . . ," Stephanie said. "I think I've got it. How about custom-printed T-shirts?"

That was how we ended up with four T-shirts from Trendy. They were bright red — Stephanie's idea, natch — with big black letters across the front that said "We're Kevin's No. 1 Fans!"

Kate had grumbled that red's her worst color, but she finally gave in. She wasn't all that interested in Kevin, but she was definitely interested in getting a close-up view of a movie camera.

Anyway, that day, the four of us were wearing

the T-shirts under our regular clothes. As soon as the final bell rang at three, we planned to take off our sweaters and uncover the T-shirts. Then we'd be all set to ride our bikes out to Chesterfield and knock Kevin DeSpain's socks off.

At exactly 3:05, Kate, Stephanie, Patti, and I were in the girls' bathroom checking out our red shirts in the full-length mirror next to the sinks, when the outer door swung open. In strolled Jenny Carlin with Angela Kemp close behind.

Jenny stopped dead when she saw us. She put her hands on her hips, and gave us the once-over. Then a smug smile spread across her face. "How . . . *quaint* you look!" she said. Angela snickered on cue.

Jenny squeezed in front of us to get to the mirror. She ran a brush through her long, dark hair a couple of times. Then she sighed and shrugged her shoulders, as though she thought she couldn't possibly look anything but fabulous, anyway. "I guess we'd better step on it, Angela," she said with her nose up in the air. "Dad's probably waiting at the side entrance, ready to drive us out to Chesterfield to meet *everyone* important."

Jenny slipped her hairbrush back into her pink

13

canvas tote, which matched her jumpsuit. Then she gave herself a final, satisfied smile in the mirror, and made her exit.

"Quaint!" Stephanie growled, reaching for the door. "I'll . . . I'll *quaint* her!" I don't usually get as upset as Stephanie does, but this time I was more than ready to back her up.

"Save your breath," Kate advised. "You'll need it to ride to Chesterfield and back."

"Yeah, who cares about Jenny Carlin?!" Stephanie told herself. "We've got better things to focus on . . . like Kevin DeSpain!"

We stuffed our sweaters into our backpacks, pulled on our jackets, and headed for the bike rack out in front of the school. We'd decided to go to Chesterfield the back way, to avoid the traffic on Route 104. To do that you ride down Hillcrest for a few blocks, and then turn left onto East Main Street. You stay on East Main all the way out of Riverhurst, when it turns into Pequontic Road, which leads straight to Chesterfield.

"I still can't believe it!" Stephanie said as we pedaled down East Main past Charlie's Soda Fountain, the bank, and Trendy. "In just a few minutes, we're actually going to see Kevin DeSpain in the fabulous flesh!"

"*My* flesh is getting goosebumps," Kate muttered. "Stop a second. I'm putting my sweater back on."

"Ka-ate!" Stephanie groaned. "We're supposed to match!"

"We can match when we get there," Kate said, braking her bike in front of Tony's Italian Kitchen. "But right now I'm freezing!"

Stephanie, Patti, and I rolled up behind her at the curb, next to Tony's delivery cycle. The smell of spaghetti sauce and garlic bread came drifting into the street. At any other time it would have lured me inside in a flash for a quick slice of double-cheese pizza, at least. I'm almost always hungry. Kate and Stephanie call me the Endless Stomach. I prefer to think of myself as just having a healthy appetite. But that day I wasn't even tempted. I was so excited about seeing Kevin that my stomach was turning flip-flops!

What would he be wearing? The brown leather jacket he has on in the poster on my bedroom wall? I wondered if he'd be taller or shorter than he looks on TV. I remembered a story Stephanie told me once about running into Bolo in a department store in the city. Bolo's the lead singer of Waxy, this California heavy-metal band we really like. I always thought Bolo was at least six feet tall and built like a wrestler,

15

but Stephanie said he was a *shrimp*! I hoped Kevin wasn't going to be too short for me. . . . But I decided he couldn't be, because his co-star Marcy Monroe used to be a model, and models have to be tall, don't they? Kevin was definitely several inches taller than Marcy. Unless he stood on a box in all their scenes together. . . .

"Lau-ren!" I heard Stephanie's voice in my ear. "Snap out of it!"

I jerked my mind back to the here and now to discover my three friends staring at me. Stephanie was tapping her foot.

"Pizza smell must be clouding her brain," Kate said with a giggle. But she was wrong, for once. It wasn't pizza — it was . . . *Kevin*!

"Do you want to see Kevin today, or not?!" Stephanie said.

Is the sky blue? I swung onto my bike and streaked up East Main Street. I didn't slow down for the others until I'd whizzed around the big curve at the edge of town.

It took us about twenty-five minutes of steady pedaling to get to Chesterfield. When you leave Riverhurst the road gets narrower and a lot of it's uphill. Patti and I are used to long, hard bike rides, but Kate and Stephanie were really panting by the time we were in sight of the ten-foot-high stone wall that surrounds the estate.

"I can't go another inch!" Kate gasped. Her face was as pink as Jenny Carlin's jumpsuit. As I said, she's really not into exercise.

Stephanie's not either. She's convinced that sweating makes her hair frizz. But she'd do anything for Kevin, even risk the frizzies. "The gate is around the corner," she puffed. "Come on, Kate — if I can make it, you can. Just a few yards more. . . ."

When we turned onto Route 104, we could hardly believe our eyes. It looked as though half the county was going to Chesterfield! Cars were lined up on both sides of the road. The Riverhurst police were doing their best to move them along, but the drivers had all slowed down to a crawl to peer through the gate.

"No stopping!" I recognized Officer Warner waving cars on. "No parking, ma'am, no exceptions!"

We pedaled carefully along the shoulder of the road to avoid the traffic jam. There were station wagons full of parents and kids. Five or six cars were crammed with girls from Riverhurst High. We spotted my brother Roger's girlfriend, Linda, smushed into the front of a green VW Beetle. There were older couples and younger couples, even a van full of older women. I halfway expected to run into my grand-mother!

"Hey, look! It's Jenny and Angela!" Kate burst into giggles. "They're stuck!"

Jenny and Angela were sitting in the back of Mr. Carlin's blue two-door sedan. The car was barely inching along, and Jenny was positively *fuming*! We could hear her screeching at her dad over the seat, even though all the windows were closed.

"Hi-i-yee, Jenny!" Stephanie called out brightly as we zipped past them. "Going someplace?" Then all four of us waved politely. Jenny's lower lip was stuck way out. She looked as if she was going to throw a temper tantrum any minute. It was excellent!

But I felt a lot less cheerful when we got even with the Chesterfield gate.

"I didn't know it *could* close!" Kate exclaimed.

Neither did I! The entrance to the main Chesterfield driveway is about twenty feet wide, with two enormous wrought-iron gates on either side that are always pushed back. At least, they'd been pushed back all the times we'd visited the house on school field trips. But that day the gates were closed tight. A young guy with messy hair and a droopy mustache sat just behind them in a folding chair. He was listening to his Walkman, and bobbing his head up and down in time to the music.

"Oh, no!" Stephanie wailed. "We can't see anything from here, and it doesn't look like there's any way to get in!"

"Kevin — so near and yet so far," Patti murmured sadly.

The young guy looked up. "Move along," he said, motioning at us.

My heart sank to my feet. "Now what do we do?" I asked.

"There are some bikes beside that maple tree straight ahead," Kate said. "Let's pull over." The tree's trunk was next to the road, but its branches spread over the fence, into forbidden Chesterfield territory.

"KH," Patti read on the license plate of the nearest ten-speed. "Isn't that Kyle's bike?" Kyle Hubbard's a guy in Mrs. Milton's class, 5A. He and Kate got to be good friends last year, when they were in the same class.

Kate nodded and looked around. "Yeah. He must be around somewhere . . . ," she began. She was interrupted by shouts from the maple tree.

"Hey, Kate!" "Lauren!" "Up here!"

Three heads popped out of the leaves about half-

19

way up the maple tree: Kyle, Mark Freedman from our class, and . . . Pete Stone!

"Ick!" I muttered. "It's Pete! I'm getting out of here!"

"What's more important, Lauren," Stephanie hissed. "Avoiding Pete, or meeting Kevin?! We have to get up there and see what's going on!" She squinted up at the boys. "Do you guys have a good view from where you are?" she called out.

"We can see all the way down to the river!" Mark yelled back.

"Great!" said Stephanie. "We're coming up!"

Chapter
3

Climbing trees is not exactly Stephanie's style, or Kate's for that matter. Patti and I had to give them both a boost to the lowest branch of the maple. Then we swung up ourselves.

Stephanie stuck one foot in a notch and pulled herself higher. But Kate grumbled, "I'll probably slip and kill myself."

"We'll grab you," I said. Patti and I were right behind her. Kate finally took a step up. "I can't believe I'm about to break my leg for Kevin DeSpain," she muttered.

Maples have sturdy, evenly spaced branches, which made the tree about as difficult to climb as a ladder. As soon as our heads were almost level with Kyle, Mark, and Pete's feet, we stopped and looked out over Chesterfield.

We were right next to the parking lot where the school buses always drop us off on field trips. That day it was jammed with cars and trucks and Winnebagos. "Each of the stars gets a Winnebago as a personal dressing room when they're on location," Kate told us.

"You mean one of those Winnebagos is Kevin's?!" Stephanie asked breathlessly.

"I wonder which?" Patti murmured longingly.

"Kevin!" Kyle Hubbard exclaimed from above us. "You mean you like Ke-vin?!" Mark Freedman made gagging noises. I was really glad that my jacket covered up my red Kevin's No. 1 Fan T-shirt!

"What's so great about him?" Pete Stone said, brushing his brown hair out of his eyes. "I think he's goofy-looking!" Pete actually thought *he* was handsomer than Kevin DeSpain?!

"Oh, yeah?" Stephanie said. "And what are you guys doing here? I'll bet you're all in love with Marcy Monroe!"

"Get real!" said Mark.

"She wears so much glop on her face, it looks like she has on a Halloween mask," Pete added. That happens to be true, and it made me think a little better of him.

"We're here because of the plane," Kyle explained. "See it over there? They landed it right on the river."

A red-and-yellow biplane floated on pontoons next to the Chesterfield dock.

"Wow!" I was looking at the *actual plane* Kevin DeSpain sits in every Tuesday night. Now *I* had goosebumps!

"Yeah, it's great, isn't it?!" Mark said in an awed voice. "It was so cool when it landed. It's a British fighter plane from World War I. It can flip and glide and — "

"You saw it land?" Stephanie shrieked. She practically fell out of the tree trying to get a better look. "Did you see Kevin get out of it?"

"Of course not!" Kate answered for them. "They'd never let a star fly a plane. That's what stunt people are for."

"Oh!" Stephanie said, disappointed. "Do you think he's down there, where the lights are?"

On the sloping stretch of lawn between the brick mansion and the river, a large group of people was milling around three huge round lights set up on tall poles.

23

"Those lights are called Fresnels," Kate said excitedly. "I've never seen any in person!"

"Why do they need light?" I asked. "The sun is shining!"

Kate shook her head. "It doesn't matter. They use the lights to get rid of any shadows that might show up on the film." I may not always agree with Kate's taste in movies — or movie stars — but she really does know a lot about movie-making. "And there's the cameraman, up on that crane with the camera."

"I don't care about the cameraman!" Stephanie wailed. "Where's *Kevin*?" She peered down at the film crew, but they were so far away from us that they were about the size of ants. The only way we could have picked out Kevin would have been if he'd started jumping up and down, or turning cartwheels.

Suddenly we heard a loud *putt-putt-putt* noise. The propeller on the biplane's nose started to spin, and the crane lifted the cameraman higher in the air.

"If they're just filming the plane landing and taking off," Kate said, "Kevin may not be here at all."

The propeller spun faster, and the plane started gliding up the river. Its pontoons made little white waves on the surface of the water.

24

Mark whistled. "Would I ever like to fly in that!"

"Outstanding!" Pete exclaimed. The plane's nose pointed toward the clouds, and it rose above the water. It didn't go far, though. The pilot made a big circle. Then the plane dropped down, and settled on the river again, floating like a feather.

"They'll probably do this for a while," Kate said. "When they make a movie they usually take lots of shots of the same scene, so they can splice together the best parts later on."

Patti nodded. "In the city I once saw a movie crew film a taxi driving up to a restaurant and stopping at the curb at least fifteen times."

"That's okay," Kyle said enthusiastically. "I could watch this all day!"

"I can't," I said, checking my watch. "I promised my mom I'd put the meat loaf in the oven at five." My mom went back to work full time a few months ago, and I often have chores to do around the house in the afternoon.

"We might as well all leave together," Kate said, with a glance at Stephanie. "I don't think we're going to see Kevin today. Either he's not around at all, or he's way down by the river with the rest of the group."

"I guess so," Stephanie agreed with a sigh. Patti nodded glumly.

"Are you riding back now?" Pete called down to us.

"Yes," Kate answered.

"I'll come with you, okay?" Pete said.

It *wasn't* okay with me, but I couldn't think of a way to tell Pete that. So Pete said good-bye to Mark and Kyle and climbed down with the four of us.

"We have to think of another way to get to Kevin," Stephanie said to me as we grabbed our bikes. "Let's use our brains. Who gets through that gate besides the movie crew?"

"We saw a delivery van from the Gilded Lobster drive in," Pete volunteered. "I guess they needed munchies."

"Very expensive munchies!" Kate said. The Gilded Lobster's just about the priciest place in town. "But I don't think they'd let you stow away, Stephanie."

We started pedaling back toward the gate. I was riding in front, followed by Pete, Patti, Kate, and Stephanie. The cars on Route 104 were still bumper-to-bumper. All of a sudden, I heard someone exclaim loudly enough to be heard over all that traffic, "This is ridiculous! I'm on the Preservation Council!"

"It's Mr. Carlin!" Patti said. He was standing in front of the gate, arguing with the guy with the mustache.

"I can't help that," the young man replied calmly. "*I'm* kind of like a preservation council myself, preserving the privacy of the people in here. And I can't let just anybody in."

"But I spoke to John Fowler, the producer! He'll tell you!" Mr. Carlin thundered, flinging his arms around. He's a small, thin man with a sharp chin, like Jenny's, and he was pointing his chin straight at the guy behind the gate.

"Fowler's in the city today," the guy said.

"Then I must insist that you . . ."

We didn't want Mr. Carlin to catch us eavesdropping, so we pedaled quickly past them. I couldn't resist glancing back over my shoulder, though. The young guy had sat down again, and he was busy adjusting the volume on his Walkman. I guess the argument was over as far as he was concerned, but Mr. Carlin seemed to be working himself into a real state. Then I turned around again, and I found myself eye-to-eye with Jenny herself!

Her dad had left the blue car on the shoulder of the road while he went over and talked to the man behind the gate. Jenny and Angela were still sitting in the back seat. Jenny was staring out the side window with a big scowl on her face. When she focused on me, riding along with Pete Stone, her eyes got rounder and rounder. Then they narrowed to slits, and she absolutely *glowered*! For a second I thought she might even stick out her tongue, but I guess her face was frozen with rage.

"Hey, Jenny!" Pete called out cheerily as we coasted past.

"Toodles!" Kate added from the end of the line.

Of course, Stephanie, Patti, Kate, and I couldn't talk about Jenny or her father in front of Pete. But as soon as he'd turned off East Main onto his street, Jagger Lane, we all burst out laughing.

"Could you believe Mr. Carlin, waving his arms around like a windmill?!" Kate sputtered.

"The poor guy was probably afraid to give Jenny the bad news," I said. Jenny's an only child, and she rules the roost in her house.

"Maybe *we* didn't meet Kevin today," Stephanie said, grinning. "But neither did Jenny, after all her bragging!"

"When she s-saw you with P-Pete, Lauren, I th-thought she was going to . . . to explode!" Patti was giggling so hard that she stammered.

"It's a good thing Jenny doesn't know how to drive, or I think she would have backed right over me with her car!" I said, giggling, too.

"*I* think Pete Stone likes you again, Lauren," Kate said.

I shook my head. "I think if he likes anyone it's you, Kate," I teased. "Remember, Kathy Simon and Barbara Paulson are both *blondes*. . . ."

"But seriously," Stephanie broke in, "we've got to do something fast. Kevin's only here for *six* more days! The *Clarion* said the movie people would be leaving on Sunday. So how do we get him to notice us when we're on the other side of a ten-foot stone wall?" She sighed loudly and pointed to the neck of her T-shirt. "I'm afraid these just won't do it."

"What about a banner?" Patti suggested. "We could paint a message to Kevin in really big letters on an old sheet or something, and hang it over the wall from the maple tree!"

"A banner?" Kate raised her eyebrows. "Isn't that sort of corny?" Like I said, she wasn't as nuts about Kevin as the rest of us.

"It's a great idea!" Stephanie exclaimed. "And maybe I could paint Kevin's face on one end of the banner. When he sees it, he'll figure if his fans have gone to that much trouble, they deserve a hello, at least!''

"What will the banner say?" I asked.

"How about, 'Kevin, We Love You, We Love You, *We Love You!*' That should get his attention," Kate joked.

Stephanie ignored her. "How about, 'Kevin, You're the Greatest!' " she said.

Patti and I nodded. "That sounds good," I said. "Patti, maybe you and Kate could be in charge of painting the letters, because your handwriting is the neatest." Stephanie's a good artist, but her writing's even messier than mine is. "We can paint the banner at my house. I'll even provide the snacks."

"Fine!" Patti said.

Kate shrugged her shoulders. "Okay." But the look on her face said, "What a waste of time!"

"We can stop at Trendy right now and buy some poster paint!" Stephanie went on. ·

"All right," I said. "But let's hurry. I don't want to have to eat *raw* meatloaf tonight!"

We steered our bikes onto the sidewalk and leaned them against the planter in front of the store. Then we pushed open the swinging door and walked inside.

Chapter
4

Trendy is small, just one room with a long counter across the back. The walls are covered floor to ceiling with posters of everybody famous you can imagine, from Chaz, the lead singer of Heat, to Ramon Seville, Kate's favorite silent movie star, who'd be about a hundred years old if he were still alive. Practically all the floor space is taken up by three long wooden tables, which are piled high with T-shirts and sweatshirts in all colors and sizes. Besides the T-shirts with stars' pictures on them, there are ones with slogans like: "Surf City, Here I Come," and "My mom went to Wonderworld, and all I got was this lousy T-shirt."

The counter at the back of the store has shelves

under it filled with baskets of buttons, and boxes of art supplies: sketch pads, pastel crayons, poster paints, and brushes. Barry Kline usually sits behind the counter next to an ironing board, where he irons on the letters for special orders. But that afternoon the store seemed to be deserted.

"He must be here," Kate said. "The door would be locked if he'd left."

"Barry?" Stephanie called out. "Barry! Are you around?"

"Coming!" A blue curtain along the back wall was shoved aside. Barry stepped through the door behind it. "What can I do for you guys today?" Barry's about my dad's age, but he sure doesn't seem like it. He has this crazy grayish beard and wears a tiny gold hoop in his right ear. He always wears T-shirts and jeans, too. And he tells all the kids to call him Barry, not Mr. Kline.

"We need a couple of big bottles of red poster paint and two good-sized brushes," Stephanie said.

"Whose is *that*?" Kate interrupted, pointing at the back wall. A dog I'd never seen before came bounding out from behind the curtain. It ran around the counter and started jumping all over us.

"I didn't know you had a dog, Barry! Down, boy! Down!" Stephanie gasped.

"I don't," Barry said. "He's a stray. He's been going through the trash cans in back for a few days now. Know anybody who might want him?"

The dog was about as tall as a German Shepherd, but he was covered with wild, curly grayish hair, almost like the hair in Barry's beard. He had shiny black eyes, and a face kind of like a sheep's. He was really pretty weird looking.

My family already has Bullwinkle, a 130-pound part-Newfoundland, and Rocky, my five-month-old kitten, so I shook my head. We don't need any more pets.

Kate, Patti, and Stephanie shook their heads, too. "I don't think my mom would go for a dog with the twins around," Stephanie said. Stephanie has a new baby brother and sister at her house.

"What do you call him?" Patti asked. She'd dug into her jacket pocket and come up with half a stick of beef jerky. The dog barely gave her a chance to get the paper off before he swallowed the jerky in a single gulp.

"Stranger," Barry replied. "Come on, boy, let's go outside and leave the customers alone." He pushed the dog through the curtain again, and disappeared after him. We heard a door slam shut, and Barry came back.

"Two big jars of red paint, and a couple of brushes?" Barry laid them out on the counter. We pooled our money to pay, and he dropped them into a paper bag.

"Any luck with your T-shirts?" he asked as we were leaving.

"No," Stephanie said, "but we're not giving up." She tapped the bag and grinned. "We've got a whole new plan."

As we headed up East Main Street, I said, "So tomorrow afternoon at my house to do the banner?" My mom doesn't mind if I have Kate, Stephanie, and Patti over when she's not home, as long as we're careful, and don't cook anything. "We have lots of old sheets," I went on. "And maybe I'll make some of Patti's Alaska Dip. . . ."

Patti groaned. "I just remembered, I can't tomorrow," she said. "I have a special meeting of the Quarks." Patti belongs to a science club for the Riverhurst Elementary kids who are super smart. "I can't miss it. Walter Williams and I are working on a project together."

"And I've got an appointment at Dr. Nadler's," Kate said. Dr. Nadler is our dentist.

"Okay, Wednesday, then. Without fail, guys!"

Stephanie said firmly. "And maybe tomorrow afternoon Lauren and I will check out Chesterfield again."

We'd turned the corner onto Hillcrest when Kate exclaimed, "I think we're being followed!" She was peering off to her left.

"By who? Where?" Stephanie, Patti, and I swiveled around, half-expecting to see Kyle, Mark . . . or maybe even Pete . . . riding up behind us.

"Over there, beside that yellow truck," Kate said. "It's Stranger!"

"Oh, no!" All four of us screeched to a stop. We waved our arms at the dog, and yelled "Shoo!" and "Go home," meaning back to Barry's. But Stranger might as well have been deaf, because he paid no attention at all. Instead, he raced across the street and flung himself at Patti, practically knocking her flat.

"He certainly likes *you*, Patti," said Stephanie as the big, funny-looking dog stood on tiptoe to lick Patti's face.

"It must be that beef jerky you fed him," I said.

"You're the dog expert, Lauren," Kate said. "How do we make him stop following us?"

I handed Kate my bike. Then I grabbed Stranger by the scruff of his neck and led him slowly back toward East Main Street. When we got to the corner

I gave him a little shove. And when the big dog acted as though he was about to turn around, I yelled, "NO!" as loud as I could.

It made me feel crummy to do it. He was so pitiful, standing there all alone, glancing over his shoulder with those large, shiny black eyes. But I made myself be firm. *"No!"* I shouted again. "Stay." Then I sprinted back to my bike. "Let's get out of here before he changes his mind!" I ordered. We raced away and didn't look back.

As I said, Stephanie's *full* of plans. And if one doesn't work out, she always has another.

Every weekday morning the four of us meet at the intersection of Pine Street and Hillcrest to ride to school together. Stephanie's usually the last to show up, but that Tuesday she was already waiting on the corner when I got there.

"I've got a great plan for us for this afternoon," she announced as soon as I'd pulled up beside her. "Remember what Kate said about dressing up?"

I stared at her suspiciously. "We're not going to rent gorilla suits, are we?" I said.

"No," Stephanie replied. "What Kate said about us being too young to be professional gardeners. That started me thinking about what we *wouldn't* be too young to be.

"Then last night I went with my dad to Romanos to buy diapers for the twins." Romanos is this huge store at the mall that sells everything from lipstick to lawn furniture. "And I saw these!" She reached into her tote and pulled out two white cotton caps. "Ta-da!"

White caps? I frowned. "We're going to pretend to be house painters?" I asked.

"No. Delivery girls!" Stephanie said.

"Delivery girls for what?" I squawked.

"Here comes Kate!" Stephanie said softly. "Hi, Kate!" she called out and added in a whisper, "I don't want to tell her about it yet. She'll just say it's another one of my harebrained schemes."

It did sound a little harebrained to *me*. But before I could mull it over, Patti came pedaling around the corner. She looked upset.

"Is something the matter?" I asked her.

"Guess who slept in our living room last night," she replied gloomily. "I'll give you a hint. He's big and tall and he has curly grayish hair."

"It's either Barry Kline . . . or Stranger!" Kate exclaimed.

"Right the second time." Patti sighed. "He didn't give up when Lauren pulled him back to East Main Street. He just got sneakier. He must have followed us all the way up Hillcrest, hiding behind cars and stuff. When I turned into my driveway, he popped out from behind the fir tree next to our house. He scared me half to death!"

"Where is he now?" Stephanie asked, glancing around a little nervously. She's not exactly wild about getting pounced on by large dogs.

"Closed up in our garage, polishing off a fourth can of Adelaide's tuna and liver," Patti replied. Adelaide is Patti's kitten, sister to my Rocky, Stephanie's Cinders, and Kate's Frederica.

The four of us started toward school. "Are you going to keep him?" I asked excitedly. I kept remembering how sad Stranger had looked when I'd left him on East Main. I hoped he'd found a home with the Jenkinses.

"No," Patti answered, "my dad's awfully allergic to dog fur. The only reason we've got Stranger right now is that Dad's away at that conference. And Horace wouldn't let Mom take him to the pound." Horace is Patti's little brother. He's really an okay kid for a six-year-old who's practically a genius.

"Maybe Stranger has an owner somewhere,"

Kate said. "Did you check out the Lost-and-Found Pets column in the *Clarion*?"

Patti nodded. "The only ad was for a missing black toy poodle answering to Fifi."

"I don't think there's any way we could make Stranger fit that description," Stephanie said thoughtfully.

We turned in at the bike rack in front of the school.

"So what are you going to do about him?" I asked.

"We have until Sunday," Patti said. "That's when Dad gets back from his conference. If we haven't found somebody to take him by then, he'll have to go to the pound." She mumbled the last words and sounded totally miserable.

Chapter
5

Stephanie didn't bring up her latest plan again that morning. She didn't mention it at lunch, either. But even if she'd decided to tell Kate and Patti about it, she wouldn't have had time to. We'd barely sat down at our table with Tuesday's Special — over-cooked hamburgers on soggy English muffins — when who should lower himself onto an empty chair across from me but . . . Pete Stone! Kyle and Mark were right behind him. I thought Jenny Carlin's eyes were going to pop out of her head!

She and Angela were sitting two tables away, close enough to hear Pete say to me, "Hey, Lauren. So, are you riding out to Chesterfield again this afternoon?"

40

"We might," I replied, flashing Pete a big smile, because I knew Jenny was watching.

"Maybe we'll ride out with you," Pete said, smiling back. Even though I was no longer interested in Pete Stone I had to admit he has a nice smile. "Right, guys?"

"Sure," Kyle said around a mouthful of burger.

"Sorry, we can't," Stephanie cut in. "We have to stop at a couple of places first." She nudged me with her elbow.

We do? What stops? I wondered to myself. But I didn't find out until three o'clock that afternoon when Stephanie and I left Kate and Patti in front of the school and started pedaling down to Main Street.

The first stop was Trendy. After we told Barry about Stranger, Stephanie asked, "Can you put letters on *caps*?"

Barry nodded. "If you've got the caps, I can decorate 'em. Let me warm up the equipment." He plugged in his iron, and pulled out a small basket filled with iron-on letters in all different colors and sizes. "I know you'll want them *red*," he said, "but what do you want them to spell?"

"Tony's," Stephanie answered promptly.

"Tony's?" I said. "Tony who?" Wasn't it *Kevin* we were interested in?

"You'll see," Stephanie replied mysteriously.

Barry quickly ironed on the red letters across the front of each cap. They looked very sporty, but I was still confused. What was Stephanie up to?

Barry handed us the caps. "Great!" Stephanie said, slipping hers on, and studying her reflection in the mirror at the end of the counter. "Thanks a lot, Barry." She turned to me. "Okay. Next stop, my dad's office." She payed Barry, stuffed the caps into her backpack, and walked out the door.

Mr. Green's a lawyer at Blake, Binder, and Rosten. He works in an office building on Main Street. I waited downstairs with the bikes while Stephanie hurried inside. She was back in no time with what looked like a large empty box wrapped in brown paper. "I got Dad to bring these to his office," she explained, "but I wrapped them up first because I didn't really want him to know what we were up to."

"What are they?"

"Cardboard boxes," said Stephanie.

I *knew* that!

Stephanie pulled down part of the brown paper. Underneath was a cardboard box, all right. But it was painted white. And in fairly neat black letters down one edge, it said, "Tony's Italian Kitchen." In the center, Stephanie had drawn a big bowl of spaghetti and meat balls!

"What are we supposed to do with *that* thing?" I asked.

"Yours is inside it," Stephanie said, taking her time answering my question. She pulled the paper down farther to show me. "It looks just like mine, only it's a tiny bit smaller. See the strings? They're so we can tie the boxes to our handlebars."

She turned the large box around, so that the open side faced the back of her bike, and rested the bottom of the box on her fender. "Then we put on the caps, and . . . Shazzam! We're delivery girls from Tony's Italian Kitchen with our delivery cycles! Now all we need is the pizza."

I was impressed. Only Stephanie could come up with a plan like that. But then I shook my head. "It'll never work," I said. "You think we'll simply ride up to the Chesterfield gate, tell the guy with a mustache that we have a delivery for Kevin DeSpain, and he'll let us in? No way!"

"Of course not, Lauren," Stephanie said impatiently. "Use your imagination!"

I wished Kate could hear Stephanie say that. Kate's always advising me to *stifle* my imagination!

"We ride up to the gate and say we have an

order for John Fowler, the producer!" Stephanie said. "That way the gate man will never suspect we're just regular old Kevin DeSpain fans, because what regular old Kevin DeSpain fans would know the producer's name? Then, once we're inside, we find Kevin's Winnebago and camp out there, if necessary, until he shows up! Pretty good, huh?"

"Not bad," I had to admit. And I still think it actually *could* have worked. . . .

We taped the brown paper wrapping back onto the big box and rode to Tony's as fast as we could. There, we ordered two double-cheese pizzas with pepperoni, meatballs, and olives — our favorites. Stephanie slid the pizzas into the big box tied to her bike. They smelled de-lic-ious!

"I had to ask Dad to advance me my allowance for the next month," Stephanie said. "But it'll all be worth it when we meet" — she rolled her eyes dreamily — "*Kevin*. . . ." She kind of sighed the last word.

When we got to the outskirts of Riverhurst, we pulled over to the side of the road and ripped the paper off the big box. Then I tied the smaller box to my bike, and Stephanie put one of the double-cheese pizzas inside it. After that we put on our caps and we were ready to go!

"Excellent!" Stephanie said. "Now, let's hustle!"

We made it to Chesterfield in record time — eighteen minutes flat. I think breathing in those pizza fumes gave us extra energy.

We turned the corner onto Route 104. The crowd was as big as it was the day before. There were wall-to-wall cars on the road — a policeman was trying to keep them moving. The young guy with the mustache was sitting on the folding chair on the other side of the closed gate. He was listening to his Walkman again, too.

Stephanie made the thumbs-up sign to me. We turned off the road onto the gravel driveway that runs through the gate to the main house. We stopped right in front of the gate, adjusted our caps, and waited for the guy to notice us. It took a while. He had his eyes closed, and he was tapping his toes, and kind of muttering along with the song he was listening to.

Finally, Stephanie yelled, "Hello?! Excuse me!"

The young guy's eyes blinked open. He pulled his headphones off and stood up. "What can I do for you?"

"Delivery for John Fowler from Tony's Italian Kitchen," Stephanie spoke right up.

"Girl delivery boys, huh?" the man said ap-

45

provingly. "Cute." He had nice blue eyes.

"Right." Stephanie pulled the pizza out of her delivery cycle, flipped back the top of the pizza box, and said, "Double-cheese with pepperoni, meatballs, and olives." Yumm! Surely a *fake* wouldn't go to that much trouble!

"Smells good," the guy said, taking a deep breath. "Okay — see that parking lot down there?"

"Yes," both of us said at once . . . he was actually reaching for the latch on the gate! He pushed it up and took a few steps back, so that he could pull the left half of the wrought-iron gate open. We were *getting in*!

Then a man's voice said grimly, "I'm here to see John Fowler AGAIN!"

"Don't turn around!" Stephanie hissed. "It's Mr. Carlin!"

"Hang on," the young guy said to us with a friendly smile. He walked around our bikes to the Carlins' car. From the sound of the engine, it was only about a foot away from our back wheels. But Stephanie and I were afraid to look, just in case Jenny was with her dad.

"I spoke to John Fowler an hour ago," Mr. Carlin continued in a loud voice. "He told me to come right out. He said he'd leave word at the gate."

46

We heard paper unfolding. The young guy had a list. "Your name is . . . ?"

"Carlin!" Mr. Carlin thundered.

"He must be alone," I was thinking, "or we would definitely have heard some squawking from Jenny by now."

"Carlin . . . Carlin . . . got it," the guy said. "Let me open the gate wider. Just go straight to the parking lot. Mr. Fowler's office is in that Winnebago at the right."

He walked around us and pushed the left half of the gate all the way open, so that Mr. Carlin could drive through. "You girls can follow him," he added to us.

I've never been so excited in my life, and I'm sure Stephanie felt the same way. We were only moments away from meeting the one, the only, Kevin DeSpain!

But then our bubble burst. "Stephanie? Lauren!" Jenny Carlin's voice screeched in my ear. "I thought it was you! What are you wearing those ridiculous caps for? Trying to sneak in to see Kevin?" She grinned spitefully out the window at us, and Mr. Carlin's car rolled past on its way up the gravel driveway.

The young man with the mustache slowly shook

his head. "Kevin DeSpain fans, huh?" he said. "Sorry, girls. Nice try. . . ." He closed the wrought-iron gate in our faces. Then he sat back down on the folding chair, and slipped on his headphones.

"Just let me get my hands on that . . . that *Carlin!*" Stephanie gurgled furiously. She grabbed the bars on the gate as if she were trying to bend them apart. "I'll . . . I'll . . ."

"Let's just go home," I murmured. I was too disappointed to think of anything comforting to say. Jenny Carlin had definitely won the second round, and that meant no Kevin DeSpain. I was so totally bummed out that I never wanted to see a double-cheese pizza with pepperoni, meatballs, and olives as long as I lived.

Chapter
6

It was already Wednesday. Two days down, four and a half to go before Kevin DeSpain left Riverhurst forever! Would the Sleepover Friends get to meet their all-time favorite movie star or not? I was pretty discouraged. In fact, the best thing that happened to me all day long was overhearing Jenny Carlin whine to Angela before classes started, "We met Mr. Fowler and some of the *workers*. But *Kevin* had an appointment in the city. Not even Marcy Monroe was there!" My arch-enemy wasn't having any better luck than I was.

Mark and Pete Stone sat at our table for lunch again, but I couldn't decide whether that was good or bad, or if I just didn't care one way or the other.

As soon as school was over for the day, I rushed

home to get ready for the banner painting. Patti was bringing over some new tapes she'd bought at the Record Emporium. Kate had made a platter of her super-fudge, and Stephanie had gotten some pictures back from Fast Fotos that she wanted to show us. But first the three of them rode home to change into painting clothes. That gave me just enough time to do the vacuuming for Mom — my chore for the day.

I was just finishing the living room when Kate and Patti rang the front doorbell.

"Isn't Stephanie here yet?" Patti asked as we trooped into the kitchen.

I shook my head. "Well, we can set up in the basement while we're waiting for her," Kate said.

I'd already piled up all the supplies we'd need on the kitchen counter: poster paints, brushes, and an old white sheet Mom said we could use. I'd also made sure we had plenty of fuel for the painters: Dr Peppers, a bowl of Patti's Alaska Dip, chips, and now Kate's super-fudge. Patti ran upstairs to my bedroom to get my cassette player. Meanwhile, Kate and I started carrying stuff down to the basement. We pushed boxes and newspapers and a broken armchair aside to make enough room to spread out the sheet. (*Some* of my messiness *is* inherited.)

"You and Stephanie really didn't say much about your trip to Chesterfield yesterday," Kate prodded me.

"Yeah. Well . . ." I grinned. "She was kind of embarrassed because her plan didn't work out. But it *almost* did."

"What was the plan?" Patti had trotted down the basement stairs, with my cassette player and her new tapes.

So I told them about the white caps with the red letters that spelled Tony's, and the fake delivery cycles, and the double-cheese pizzas with pepperoni, meatballs, and olives.

Kate burst out laughing. "Only Stephanie could have come up with something as crazy and complicated as that! She'd do *anything* to meet Kevin!"

"So what happened?" Patti asked.

I told them about running into Jenny Carlin at the gate and how she'd totally blown our cover. Just talking about it made me mad all over again.

"That Jenny Carlin can be just so . . . so plain mean!" Patti said.

Kate nodded in agreement. "We're going to make this the best banner ever!" she said, sounding absolutely determined. "Now even *I* want to meet

Kevin DeSpain, just to show up Jenny Carlin!"

I glanced down at my watch. "I wonder why Stephanie's so late?"

"Stephanie's always late," Kate pointed out. "Let's get started without her. She'll paint the face in last, anyway."

Kate and Patti had decided to outline the letters on the banner first. Then we could all take turns filling them in with red poster paint.

I found some pencils and a couple of rulers in my dad's desk. Then we stretched the sheet tight on the basement floor, and weighted it down at the corners with books. Patti popped Heat's latest cassette into the player and turned it up loud. And she and Kate got to work. While they sketched in the first line of the banner — an enormous "KEVIN" — Patti told us how Stranger was doing.

"He really *is* sweet," she reported. "He has this cute way of cocking his head at you when you talk to him. And he's very smart, too. He already answers to his name. He comes whenever I call him, and Horace is teaching him to sit."

"Horace likes him?" Kate said. Up till then, Horace mainly seemed interested in his collection of creepy-crawlies — turtles, a couple of lizards, a salamander, even a garter snake. To my mind, a dog would be a real improvement.

Patti nodded. "He's nuts about Stranger. He worries that we're not feeding the dog enough, and is always nagging Mom to buy him more food — meanwhile, Stranger's eating us out of house and home. Horace is also really afraid that we won't be able to find Stranger someone nice to live with before Sunday . . ."

"Who have you talked to about taking Stranger?" I asked.

"Mom's been asking everywhere at the university," Patti said. "She's told all of her classes about him, and everyone at the faculty club. She's put notices on every bulletin board, with a short paragraph about what Stranger's like and what a great pet he'd make — it's got our name and telephone number at the bottom. Maybe somebody will call."

"I can have my mom and dad ask at their offices," I said.

"And Dad can mention him at the hospital," Kate added. She'd put on her glasses to work on the banner, and she was frowning down at the huge, swirly "K" she was drawing.

"That would be great," Patti said. "Of course,

Horace is hoping no one will be interested, and that Mom will break down and let us keep Stranger. This morning at breakfast, Horace told me about a program he'd watched on TV about lost animals. He kept talking about how we had to get Stranger a collar with a special metal dog tag with our name, number, and address on it, so he can be returned." Patti shook her head and sighed. "Horace asked me how much I thought that would cost. He wants to start saving his allowance to get one for Stranger as soon as Mom decides to let us keep him."

"Poor little guy," I said. "Is there really no chance you might be able to?"

"No chance," Patti said. "A dog within three miles makes my dad's head stuff up completely."

While Kate finished outlining the K, Patti lay down on her stomach and drew in the smaller E, V, I, and N.

Kate and Patti had just finished the first line — the "Kevin" with a long dash after it — when I heard Bullwinkle's muffled barking. I'd locked him up in the upstairs spare bedroom, because trying to get anything done with Bullwinkle around is like trying to play ping-pong in a hurricane.

"Turn off the tape," I said to Kate, since it was

closest to her. "Maybe it's the doorbell."

But it wasn't. It was the telephone. I don't know how many times it had already rung. By the time I'd thundered up the basement stairs to the wall phone next to the fridge, whoever was calling had given up. I puttered around the kitchen long enough to pile a tray with the drinks and snacks, thinking the caller might try again. Then I carried them down to the basement. Kate and Patti had already finished the second line — "You're the" — and started on the third — "Greatest!"

"Nobody there," I said, setting the tray down on the broken armchair. I handed each of them a tall glass of cold Dr Pepper.

"If Stephanie doesn't show up soon, maybe we should call *her*," Patti suggested.

"Good idea," Kate said. And that's just what we did.

Mrs. Green answered, which sort of surprised me, because I'd dialed Stephanie's private line. I could hear one of the twins crying in the background.

"Mrs. Green? This is Lauren," I said. "I hope I didn't wake the babies up." I held the phone away from my ear, so that Kate and Patti could hear Mrs. Green, too.

55

"Oh, hello, Lauren. No, Jeffrey's just yelling for his dinner," Mrs. Green replied. "I picked up because I thought it might be one of you girls. Didn't Stephanie get you?"

"No, she didn't. We were wondering when she's coming over to my house . . . ," I said.

"I don't really know," said Mrs. Green. "Her dad drove up just as Stephanie got home from school. He said he had something urgent he wanted to show her."

"Oh." Was Stephanie in some kind of trouble? The last time my parents had something urgent they wanted to show me, it was a C on my report card!

"A surprise," Mrs. Green added helpfully.

"Oh!" I said again. Mr. Green is always coming up with terrific surprises for Stephanie. For her birthday this year, he gave her a little house in the backyard. Not bad, huh? He calls it "Stephanie's cottage." He had it built at the same time as he had the new wing added onto the main house for the twins.

The cottage is really neat. It has pull-out couches for overnights, a small refrigerator for munchies, and a color TV. We almost always stay there when we sleep over at the Greens'. I wondered what Mr. Green could possibly come up with to top that!

56

I guess Mrs. Green wondered, too, because she added, "*I* don't even know what the surprise is."

"Well, thank you. Say hello to the babies for me," I told her and hung up.

"I'll bet Stephanie's dad'll drop her off when they're through," Patti murmured.

"He'd better!" Kate said. "If *I* try to draw Kevin's face, he'll end up looking like Mr. Potato Head."

We trooped back down to the basement and started filling in the letters with paint. I expected Stephanie to ring the doorbell any second and come rushing in to show us her surprise.

"Maybe it's those black leather sneakers we saw at the mall last weekend," Kate said.

"Or maybe her dad finally agreed to let her get her ears pierced," Patti guessed. "And he bought her some earrings."

But we finished the letters and the snacks, washed off the paint brushes and ourselves, and we still hadn't heard a word from Stephanie.

"I've got to go home," Kate said at last. "Dad's cooking something new tonight. You know how upset he gets if we're not there the second he takes it out of the oven." Dr. Beekman is a fabulous cook. I can personally vouch for the fact that the Beekmans have the world's best leftovers in their refrigerator.

"I have to go, too," Patti said. "A visiting professor's coming for dinner tonight."

"Maybe the professor will take Stranger," I said.

Patti grinned. "She's from China."

"Then maybe she'll want Stranger as an outstanding example of an all-American dog?" I suggested hopefully.

We all glanced at our banner one last time. I thought we'd done a fantastic job. It was neat, colorful, and best of all, the letters were *huge*.

"Kevin won't need his bionic powers to see this one," I said, feeling truly satisfied with our work. "Should I fold it up when it's dry and bring it to school in the morning?"

"Why don't we just leave it where it is?" Patti said. "Tomorrow we can race over here as soon as classes are finished, and Stephanie can add in the face with quick-drying marker."

"Call if you hear from her," Kate said as we headed up the basement stairs again.

"You, too," I replied.

But Mom, Dad, Roger, and I went out to dinner at Burger Joint. We got back kind of late, so I had no idea if Stephanie had phoned anybody or not.

Chapter
7

"Stephanie didn't call me last night!" was the first thing Kate said when we met on the corner on Thursday morning.

"Me, neither," Patti said.

"And where is she now?" Kate added crossly, looking down at her watch. "It's already eight thirty-four! We'll miss the first bell, and if we don't step on it, we'll miss the second one, too!"

The bell to go into the school building rings at eight thirty-five. The second bell rings at eight forty-five. And if you're not in your seat then, you're doomed!

"Oh, nooooo! Not another lunch date with Mrs. Wainwright!" I moaned. "Let's get moving!" Mrs. Wainwright's the principal at Riverhurst Elementary.

If you're late more than once, you have to spend lunch hour *in her office*! It's really not a lot of fun. Mrs. Wainwright has a stare that can practically freeze your blood, and she's quick to use it!

We made it to Mrs. Mead's room with about two and a half minutes to spare. But Stephanie cut it a lot closer than that. She slid into her desk not thirty seconds before the late bell rang! Although Kate and I sit right behind her, she didn't turn around to whisper anything to us, either. Instead she sat up very straight in her chair, faced the front, and opened her math notebook before Mrs. Mead had even asked us to. This wasn't typical Stephanie behavior at all!

As soon as Mrs. Mead sent Mark Freedman and Robin Becker to the board to do some of our math homework problems, Kate nudged the back of Stephanie's chair with her toe. "Where were you yesterday?" she hissed.

Stephanie still didn't turn around. "Tell you later," she muttered over her left shoulder.

And we couldn't get another word out of her all morning, not even when Mrs. Mead was scolding Henry Larkin at the front of the room for goofing off, and practically everyone else in the class was whispering, passing notes, and giggling.

At lunchtime Stephanie bolted out of her chair and practically raced to the cafeteria. But Kate, Patti, and I were close behind. We joined her in the line.

"Now we can talk," I said to Stephanie. "So come on. . . . What was your dad's big surprise?"

Stephanie glanced around kind of nervously, "I don't want to talk about it here. Uh . . . okay? Wait until we . . . uh . . . we sit down," she fumbled. Kate, Patti, and I exchanged glances. Just what was the big secret?!

But we waited until all four of us had sat down at our regular table. Patti, Kate, and I waited expectantly. Stephanie swallowed a couple of times.

"Hurry up and tell us!" Kate urged. "Before Pete Stone decides he just *has* to have lunch with Lauren again."

"Well . . ." Stephanie said. "I had no idea where Dad wanted to take me, right?" She paused.

"Right," I said. "Go on."

"So we got into his car and drove to West Main Street," Stephanie said, "to that new office building next to the health club. . . ." Then she stopped as if she'd run out of steam again.

"Your dad has a new office?" Patti guessed helpfully.

"He's not working for Blake, Binder, and Rosten any more?" asked Kate. What kind of a surprise was that?!

"No, no. . . ." Stephanie shook her head. "I'm . . . I'm trying to tell you, if you'll just give me a chance."

Stephanie usually loves surprises, but she didn't seem to be enjoying this one very much.

"We got out of the car, walked into the building," Stephanie said, "and. . . ."

"Stephanie!" Kate groaned.

". . . took the elevator to the eighth floor." Stephanie finished her sentence. Her cheeks were starting to turn bright pink. I couldn't understand what was the matter with her. "Then we turned right and went down a long hall, to a door that said — "

"Stephanie! Was yesterday fabulous or what?" someone screeched practically in my ear.

I almost *croaked*! It was the dreaded Jenny Carlin!

"Kevin was even better-looking than he is on TV, didn't you think?" Jenny shrieked even louder for the benefit of every kid in the cafeteria.

"Better!" echoed her sidekick, Angela Kemp.

Kate was quicker on the uptake than I was. I was still trying to get my mind around the fact that

Jenny Carlin seemed to be having a conversation —
a friendly conversation — with somebody *at our
table*!

"Better-looking than he is on TV!" Kate said in
a stern voice. "That was your surprise? You saw Kevin
DeSpain *in person*, Stephanie?!"

Patti and I stared at Stephanie, absolutely
speechless.

"Of course she did," Jenny Carlin said. A cat-
ate-the-canary smile spread across her face. "We
drove out to Chesterfield together, didn't we, Stephanie? It was *terrific*!" She drew out the last word as
long as she possibly could.

Stephanie just blinked a couple of times and
looked sort of sick.

"Well, if you had such a good time together
yesterday," Kate said, "I definitely think you deserve
to have lunch together *today*!"

She stood up and picked up her tray. "Come
on, guys," Kate said to Patti and me. Then she
marched across the cafeteria to a table in the corner.

"Stephanie . . . ?" Patti said, still not wanting
to believe it.

Stephanie shrugged her shoulders a little. She
looked almost ready to cry.

I remembered what Kate had said about Stephanie being willing to do *anything* to meet Kevin DeSpain. She'd done *anything*, all right! She'd actually joined forces with my worst enemy in the whole world!

I grabbed my tray and followed Kate. Patti wasn't far behind me.

Chapter
8

Afternoon classes were a total blur that day. On the one hand, I wanted to ask Stephanie a million questions about Kevin: Are his eyes as green as they look on TV? Is he short or tall? What was he wearing? Was he nice? What did he say to you? What did you say to him? Did you get his autograph?

On the other hand, I never wanted to *talk* to Stephanie again! I could see *yelling* at her maybe, like: "How could you have gone without us?" and more important "How could you have gone *anywhere* with Jenny Carlin?!" But it's impossible to start yelling in the middle of class — especially Mrs. Mead's class. So instead, I just sat there, boring two holes in the back of Stephanie's head with my eyes.

When the bell rang at the end of the day, Stephanie whirled around in her seat. "Listen, guys," she began, "you have to understand that . . ."

But I was out of that room before she had time to say another word!

Kate and Patti caught up with me at the bike rack. "Practicing for the hundred-meter dash?" Kate gasped, trying to catch her breath.

"What else did Stephanie have to say?" I asked as I unlocked my bike.

"Who listened?" said Kate.

Patti shook her head gloomily. "Are we still going out to Chesterfield?" she wanted to know. I could tell she felt bad about the fight. Patti hates arguments. But this time even she thought Stephanie had gone too far.

"You bet!" I said grimly.

"Maybe we'll get lucky," Kate said.

"And if we don't, at least we'll know that *we* didn't sell out to Jenny Carlin," I muttered.

Kate and I rode to my house to pick up the banner. Patti said she'd meet us there. She had to stop off at home first, to show Stranger to a graduate student who was interested in adopting a dog.

"I hope it doesn't take her too long," Kate said, staring up at the sky as we turned onto Pine Street.

"It's kind of cloudy. If it really clouds up, they might stop filming, and if they stop filming . . ."

"Kevin might go back to the city," I finished glumly. "Why not? Everything else has gone wrong!"

"We can't give up *now*," Kate said. "Let's get that banner!"

We ran down to the basement, folded up the banner, and squeezed it into my backpack. Then we waited for Patti in the driveway. I sort of hoped we'd see Stephanie riding home, so we could ignore her. But only Patti showed up, and the three of us started on our regular route to Chesterfield.

"Did the graduate student want Stranger?" I asked Patti as we whizzed down Hillcrest.

"No." Patti shook her head. "She said he was too big." She sighed. "The guy who came by last night said he was too lively. And Mom showed him to someone yesterday afternoon who said he was too *curly*! It's already Thursday, and we haven't had any results, just a few nibbles."

We'd almost reached the end of East Main Street where it turns into Pequontic Road, when I spotted the dog. "Patti, I think Stranger's following us again," I exclaimed.

"Oh, no!" Patti wailed, pulling over. "Where is he?"

"Skulking along behind those bushes," I said. "See him?"

"Stranger, come here right this second!" Patti ordered. The fuzzy gray dog bounded cheerfully over to us. His tail was wagging like crazy. "He must have pushed the garage door open somehow," Patti murmured as he tried to lick her face. "Or crawled out through the window." She looked down at the dog. *"What* am I going to do with you?" she said.

"We can't take him back to your house," Kate pointed out. "We're running out of time." She glanced up at the clouds again.

"You guys had better go on without me," Patti said miserably.

"Absolutely not," I said. "All for one and one *for all*, right?" If only Stephanie had remembered that!

"Right," Kate agreed. "Stranger will just have to come."

So there were four of us on our way to Chesterfield after all — only one of us just happened to have four legs.

Stranger was pretty well-behaved, though. He stayed safely on the shoulder of the road next to our bikes. He wasn't even freaked out by all the traffic on Route 104. He did get a little *too* interested in the guy behind the wrought-iron gate. But we got past that, and when we reached the maple tree, Stranger lay down at the foot of it in the shade and fell sound asleep.

Patti watched him worriedly. "He'll be fine," I told her. "He's not going anywhere."

That day we had the tree to ourselves. Most of the fifth-grade boys were still at school, because tryouts had started for the baseball team. We leaned our bikes against the trunk of the maple and started climbing. Patti and I pulled ourselves up first. Then we gave Kate our hands and dragged her up to the lowest branch.

I climbed about halfway up the tree, high enough to see past the brick mansion to the river. "They've set up in the gardens today," I reported. Four of the huge round lights were pointed at a hedge trimmed into animal shapes. Once again the cameraman was raised way up in the air on his crane.

"Aren't they farther away than they were last time?" Patti asked doubtfully. "How are they ever going to see us, or even the banner?"

"They'll be walking back and forth to the Winnebagos," Kate said to cheer us up. "And I'm sure someone will tell Kevin about the banner."

I climbed down to a lower branch so Kate and

Patti could pull the banner out of my backpack. We shook it out so that it would hang straight. Then we carefully draped it over the far side of the tall stone wall.

"It looks outstanding!" Kate said. I had to agree. The white sheet really stood out against the reddish-brown stone wall. And the red letters jumped out at you, almost like neon lights: "Kevin — You're the Greatest!" He just *had* to see it!

Suddenly Patti said, "Wow — I didn't realize it was so late. It's getting dark already."

"It's not late!" Kate said. "It's the clouds."

We peered through the maple leaves at the sky. The light-gray clouds had turned to an ugly grayish-black, and they were piling up overhead.

"It looks like it might actually" — Kate stuck her hand out of the tree into the open air, left it there for a second — "*rain!*" As soon as she said it, I heard pitter-patter sounds all around, and I saw that the sleeve of Kate's jacket was spotted with big, wet drops.

Before I could climb any higher to see if the movie crew had stopped filming, the sky absolutely cracked open, and the rain came pouring down in buckets!

"This is good news, in a way," Kate said calmly

70

as water dripped off our noses and trickled down our necks. "Kevin will *have* to go to his dressing-room now, and he'll spot the banner himself!"

"He may see it, but he won't be able to read it," Patti said mournfully.

"What do you mean?" I asked.

"Poster paints run in water," she replied glumly.

I hung out of the tree more or less upside-down to take a look at our banner. And sure enough, our beautiful letters had melted into a horrible, streaky, red mess.

Kate groaned. "That does it," she said. "We might as well go home."

"The perfect end to a perfect day," I muttered as I slid soggily down the trunk. My feet hit the ground with a depressing *squish*. But the day wasn't over yet.

"Where's Stranger?" Patti exclaimed.

Our bikes were still leaning against the tree, but the big curly-haired dog was gone!

"Stranger!" we shouted into the rain. "Here, Stranger!" But there was no sign of him. In fact, there was no sign of anybody. The guy guarding the gate had disappeared. The gate was locked, and the policemen who'd been directing traffic were gone. There was no traffic to direct, anyway. All the sightseers had left as soon as the rain started.

And finally we gave up and decided to go home, too. "I'll bet someone in one of the cars took Stranger back to town, Patti," Kate said.

"That's right," I agreed. "They felt sorry for him, standing around in the rain, and loaded him into their back seat. Stranger's probably found an owner for himself. That's what we wanted, right?"

"I guess so. . . . Poor Horace," Patti said sadly. Horace wasn't the only one who'd gotten attached to the big, funny-looking dog.

"Maybe Stranger went back to your house on his own, and he'll be waiting for you when you get there," Kate said. "In either case, he had more sense than we did. I'm completely soaked!"

So we got on our bikes and started pedaling slowly back toward Riverhurst.

Chapter 9

Stranger did *not* go back to the Jenkinses' house on Thursday. When I called that evening, Patti said Horace was taking it better than she expected. "He's convinced the dog will turn up again," she said quietly. "I hope he's right." She also said she hadn't heard a word from Stephanie. And Stephanie certainly didn't try to phone me.

I met Kate at the end of her driveway the next morning. Neither of us had much to say. Silently, we rode together toward the corner of Hillcrest. The last person I expected to see there was Stephanie. I mean, it was early, and she's almost always late. But, more important, how could she possibly have the nerve after what had happened?!

But there Stephanie was, in her black leather

jacket with the red trim, watching us pedal toward her.

Kate stiffened. "We'll ride on past her," she murmured out of the side of her mouth.

But Stephanie wouldn't let us. She pushed her bike into the street in front of us. "Hold it right there!" she yelled. And she sounded *mad*, not sorry!

Kate and I stopped our bikes about five feet away from her and just sat there, not opening our mouths.

"I know what you've been thinking," Stephanie said. "You've been thinking, 'That creep Stephanie couldn't wait to sneak off without us to meet Kevin DeSpain,' haven't you?"

No answer was needed for *that* one.

"Well, you're wrong!" Stephanie declared. "It wasn't like that at all. My dad wanted to give me a nice surprise. And he just happens to be the lawyer for Mr. Pearson, the president of the First National Bank of Riverhurst." She paused for a second to catch her breath, then hurried on. "Mr. Pearson also happens to be president of the Riverhurst Association for the Preservation of Historic Homes. And Dad asked him if he could possibly fix it so I could meet Kevin DeSpain. Dad didn't know Mr. Pearson had arranged it through Mr. Carlin until we showed up at the Association office and the Carlins were there!"

Patti had coasted around the corner on her bike, and come to a screeching halt on the far side of Stephanie.

"So why didn't you say 'no thanks' when you found out?" I asked her.

"Yeah, Stephanie," Kate sniffed. "I wouldn't *cross the street* with Jenny Carlin!"

"Do you think I wanted to go with her?!" Stephanie exclaimed. "But think how bad it would have made my dad look if I'd said 'no way!' in front of Mr. Pearson, who'd gone to all that trouble to arrange it?"

Kate raised her eyebrow. "Don't raise that eyebrow at me, Kate Beekman!" Stephanie said. "What about all the times you've had to be nice to those horrible little Norwood boys, just because their dad is a doctor at Central County Hospital with your dad?" Stephanie takes after her father. She really knows how to state her case. In fact, she'd make a good lawyer. "And what about you, Lauren, having to ask Ginger Kinkaid to a sleepover when you didn't even know her, just because she happens to be Mr. Blaney's niece?" My dad works at Blaney Real Estate.

Stephanie zipped her jacket up and down angrily a few times and glared at Kate and me. "You guys are being really unfair, focusing on the *Kevin* part of it!" she said angrily. "I *had* to do it because of my dad! And anyway, Jenny Carlin has ruined Kevin DeSpain for me forever!" Her lower lip quivered a little, but she grabbed it with her teeth.

Then she pushed the pedals of her bike down so hard that she scattered gravel over half of Pine Street, and rode off, leaving the three of us sitting there, staring after her.

"Well?" I said to Kate. I felt kind of bad. Stephanie had a point. I could think of plenty of times when I'd had to do something I wasn't too wild about to help out a parent. It sounded like that was mostly what the trip to Chesterfield was about for Stephanie. Especially if she hadn't even been able to enjoy meeting Kevin. . . .

"Maybe we jumped to some conclusions," Kate said.

Patti pushed her bike over to us. "Maybe we were totally *wrong!*" she corrected Kate.

"And maybe we'll be late!" I yelped. "It's eight thirty-four again!"

"I think we have to apologize," Patti said, after we'd shot down the slope on Hillcrest and skidded to a stop at the elementary school bike rack.

"We'll talk to Stephanie at lunch," Kate said.

When the lunch bell rang, though, we lost

Stephanie between Mrs. Mead's room and the cafeteria. "She must be out in the new art studio with Ms. Gilberto," Patti said.

Ms. Gilberto's our art teacher. She's been letting some of her best students help her set up the new studio. She brings in sandwiches, and they eat lunch while they try to decide which painting or photograph looks better on which wall, and where the pottery kiln should go, and so on.

Stephanie gave us the slip after school, too. Since she sits in the front row, she's usually first out of the room when the final bell rings. But that Friday she absolutely raced to the bike rack. I might have been able to catch her before she got her bike unlocked, though, if Pete Stone hadn't stopped me halfway down the sidewalk.

Kate and Patti came scooting up behind me just in time to hear him say, "There's something I've been wanting to ask you, Lauren."

"Yes?"

I felt Kate's finger poke me in the back.

Pete cleared his throat and looked uncomfortable.

I guess he *is* interested in me again, I thought. And he wants to meet me at the movies tomorrow or at the Pizza Palace at the mall. . . .

It was kind of flattering. And it didn't hurt that Jenny Carlin's head almost swiveled off her neck as she and Angela passed by on their way to Mrs. Kemp's station wagon.

It *would* be nice to be asked even though I wasn't sure yet if I would say yes, or turn him down flat. "What is it, Pete?" I said as sweetly as I could. He was wearing the sweatshirt that I like a lot, the one with thick green and blue stripes.

"Would you . . . uh . . . would you . . ."

Here it comes, I said to myself.

The words tumbled out all at once. "Would you consider trying out for the Riverhurst Elementary School baseball team?" Pete Stone said.

The *baseball team*?!

"We could really use your pitching arm!" Pete said.

Have you ever heard of anything less romantic in your life? Pete Stone was trying to make a date with my *pitching arm*! And by the time Kate and Patti had gotten over the giggles, Stephanie was almost to Pine Street.

The sleepover was at Patti's house that Friday. My dad drove Kate and me over. The second we rang the doorbell, the Jenkinses' front door flew open, and Horace was standing there, staring up at us hopefully.

He's a thin little kid with big hands and feet, and serious greenish-brown eyes like Patti's. "Oh, it's just you," Horace said glumly. Then his lips turned down at the corners, and his shoulders slumped. Without another word, he scuffed slowly back down the hall toward the den.

" 'It's just you'!" Kate repeated. "Some friendly greeting!"

"Nothing personal." Patti had hurried downstairs to meet us. "He's still expecting someone to bring Stranger back."

As we followed Patti upstairs to her bedroom, she added, "I called Stephanie earlier."

"What did she say?" I asked.

"I didn't get *her*." Patti frowned. "I got a message: 'Hello, this is Stephanie Green's line. Please leave your name and number, and the time you called, and I *might* get back to you sometime.' "

Kate sighed. "I guess she borrowed her dad's answering machine, just so she wouldn't have to talk to us."

"It really feels weird, having a sleepover without her," I said, setting my backpack down on Patti's double bed. I was still jealous that Stephanie had met Kevin, but I was ready to admit we'd been too hard on her.

"Mom went to Sun Luck's for take-out Chinese food," Patti said. Unlike Dr. Beekman, Mrs. Jenkins is *not* very interested in cooking. "After we eat, why don't we try Stephanie again?"

"Hey! There's the phone now!" I said. "Maybe she's calling *us*!"

"I'll get it!" Patti yelled to Horace. She lunged for the phone in the upstairs hall.

But Horace got to the downstairs phone first. "Hello?" we heard him say. "Uh-huh . . . uh-huh . . . uh-huh! You *do*?! . . . Great! See you soon!"

"Who was that?" Patti called down when he'd hung up.

"Stranger's coming back!" Horace shouted up the stairs. "I knew he would!"

"How did that happen?" I said to Patti. "How could anyone know where to bring the dog?"

"Maybe they recognized him from his description on one of the bulletin boards at the university?" she said, puzzled. "But now we really have a problem," she added gloomily. "Only a day and a half to find him a place to live."

And only a day and a half until Kevin DeSpain

leaves Riverhurst for good, I thought to myself. We hadn't biked out to Chesterfield that Friday afternoon because it was raining again. And there probably wasn't any point in riding out Saturday — it was sure to be a total zoo, with just about every person in Jefferson County on Route 104. And we didn't have Stephanie to come up with a plan for us.

Mrs. Jenkins brought back egg rolls and mooshu pork and chicken in orange sauce and lots of other stuff. We'd just started opening the containers in the kitchen when the doorbell rang.

"It's him!" Horace squealed. "It's Stranger!"

"I don't want you to be too disappointed, honey," Mrs. Jenkins warned as she followed him into the hall. "But we can't keep the dog. If we're lucky, maybe we can talk this person into giving him a good home. . . ."

"Let's just stay here," Patti whispered to Kate and me. "I hate to see Horace get upset."

We dumped ice into glasses and poured in cherry soda. We were purposely not paying any attention to the conversation at the front door, but we heard footsteps coming toward the kitchen. "Girls," Mrs. Jenkins said, "there's someone here you might like to see. . . ."

I turned quickly around, thinking that maybe it

was Stephanie. Then I came as close as I've ever been in my life to *fainting dead away*!

There, in the middle of Mrs. Jenkins' kitchen, wearing sunglasses and his brown leather jacket, was the one . . . the only . . . KEVIN DESPAIN!

Did you ever play that game when you were little where you spin around really fast, or jump up and down, or just act crazy in general? Then whoever is *It* yells, "Freeze!" and you have to stop in whatever position you're in and stay that way? That's what Kate, Patti, and I were like for at least twenty seconds.

I froze in a half-turn, holding a glass of ice-cubes, with a silly apologetic grin on my face just in case it really *was* Stephanie. Patti froze with her mouth open and her forehead all wrinkled, the way it always is when she's worried — she'd been about to say something else about Horace.

But Kate was the worst of all. She froze with a container of Chinese food in each hand and a package of chopsticks clutched between her teeth!

"This is Kevin DeSpain," Mrs. Jenkins said. *As if we didn't know!!!* "Mr. DeSpain, I'd like you to meet my daughter, Patti, and two of her best friends, Lauren and Kate."

"Please call me Kevin," he said to Mrs. Jenkins in this warm, low voice. Then he stretched out his hand. "Hello," he said to us, smiling that slow smile I've seen a hundred times on TV and *never* gotten tired of. "Patti, I've come to ask you a favor."

"Y-yes . . ." Patti forced her frozen lips to move enough to form the word.

"I understand Ace is your dog," he said. Ace? I unlocked my eyes long enough to see Kevin pointing at Stranger, who was sitting next to Horace on the hall rug.

My mind was reeling! Kevin DeSpain was only three feet away from me in the Jenkinses' house, talking to us about Stranger! I secretly pinched my arm, just to make sure I wasn't dreaming. Kevin is even more fabulous in real life than he is on the screen. His hair has sun-streaks in it that don't show up on TV, and he's plenty tall, definitely over six feet.

"He . . . he's a stray. He f-followed me home," Patti had actually managed to make a sentence.

"I wondered if you'd consider giving him to me?" Kevin said, glancing at the big dog fondly. "I found him under my Winnebago yesterday after-noon, and we've been together ever since."

Give Kevin DeSpain Stranger?! I didn't know about Patti, but I'd be willing to give him Bullwinkle, my family's beloved pet! In fact, I'd probably even give Kevin my brother *Roger* if he asked for him!

"The weather's supposed to be bad for the next four or five days," Kevin went on. "Rainy and wet. So we're going to pack up tomorrow and fly back to California."

Kate, Patti, and I nodded like puppets.

"We think we have enough outdoor shots of Chesterfield already," he explained. "And we can shoot the indoor stuff on a soundstage. There's just one problem. . . ." He smiled again, and I think all three of us — and possibly even Mrs. Jenkins — sighed. *I* certainly did, anyway, I couldn't help myself.

"The problem is Ace. I don't want to leave him behind if I don't have to. He's a great dog, and I think he's gotten pretty attached to me, too, haven't you, boy?" Stranger had wandered into the kitchen and was leaning against Kevin's faded jeans.

"So-o-o . . . ," Kevin drawled, fixing his green eyes on Patti, who looked like she was in shock. "What do you say?"

"S-sure!" Patti stammered.

"Horace?" said Mrs. Jenkins.

"I guess so . . ." Horace sighed. "If *I* can't keep him."

Mrs. Jenkins shook her head. "You know how allergic your father is," she said softly.

"O-kay," Horace agreed at last.

"Terrific!" Kevin said. "I'll write the two of you at least once a month, letting you know how he's doing, okay?"

Patti, Kate, and I looked at each other and grinned. All ri-i-ight! Kevin DeSpain as a pen pal!

Then Kevin glanced over at the collection of Chinese food containers on the kitchen counter. "Chinese take-out? My favorite," he said.

"Would you like to have dinner with us?" Mrs. Jenkins offered. "I always order too much."

"Please?" Horace begged him. "That way I can play with Stranger — I mean Ace — a little longer." Maybe *we* were flipping out over Kevin, but to Horace he was just another grown-up.

"Well, I'm supposed to be meeting my producer," he began, "but I'm sure he won't mind."

"Tough darts to you, Jenny Carlin!" I said to myself. "I guess you won't be having 'Friday dinner with Kevin' after all."

"We have to call Stephanie!" Patti whispered to me as Kevin followed Horace and the gray dog into the living room. "Or she'll never forgive us."

85

"I'll do it," I said. I dialed the Greens' regular number, not Stephanie's private line. Mr. Green picked up.

"Hello, Mr. Green?" I said. "It's Lauren. I have to talk to Stephanie, *please*. Tell her if she doesn't talk to me, she'll be sorry for the rest of her life."

"That sounds serious," Mr. Green said. "I'll get her right away."

A few seconds later, I heard a cross, "What?!" It was Stephanie.

"Stephanie, there's no time to run through whose at fault," I said. "You have to come over to Patti's as fast as you can. Kevin DeSpain is here!"

"Don't get cute with me, Lauren," Stephanie growled. "I'm *not* in the mood."

"If I'm not telling the truth, you can have my autographed poster of him," I said.

"What?!" Stephanie squealed. Now she *knew* I was serious! "I'll be there in five minutes."

It was easily the most exciting night of my life!

Kevin stayed until ten-thirty, and we found out all kinds of things about him that you never read in fan magazines. He told us that he grew up on a farm in Ohio. And he has three little sisters, named Kerry, Kathleen, and Karen. Kathleen and Karen are identical twins and they're eleven years old, the same as us. And the real reason Kevin wears sunglasses a lot of the time is that he's near-sighted, just like Kate.

Kevin was totally great. We took about four dozen Polaroids of ourselves with him, first of each of us with Kevin, and then of all four of us with him. He autographed most of the photos, and even some white T-shirts that had belonged to Mr. Jenkins. Mrs. Jenkins donated them for the occasion.

Finally Kevin said he'd better go, because he was staying at a hotel in the city and he had a long drive ahead of him. But he actually invited us to *visit* him any time we were in California.

"I have a little ranch not far from San Francisco," he said. "I hope Ace will like it." Then he *kissed us all good-bye,* on the cheek!

It was fabulous! But just about as wonderful was the fact that the Sleepover Friends were *friends* again.

"I'll never wash the left side of my face as long as I live," Stephanie exclaimed as we trudged up the stairs to Patti's room.

"Me, neither," I said. "How did he ever know where to call about the dog?"

"You were on the phone when we found out," Kate said. "It was Horace."

"Horace?" I repeated.

"Remember what I told you about Horace saving up to buy Stranger a special dog tag?" Patti said. "Since he couldn't afford a real one, he did the next best thing. He made one out of cardboard paper and tape and tied it around Ace's neck with some of Mom's gray yarn. He wrote our address and telephone number on it in permanent marker. But Ace is so furry that Kevin didn't even notice it until this evening."

"Hooray for Horace!" Stephanie said. "I'm going straight to the mall tomorrow, to Feathers and Fins, to buy him the creepiest, crawliest thing they've got."

"Yeah," Kate said thoughtfully. "We could stop off at Sight 'n' Style, too, maybe, and if Mom says it's okay, I'll order some new glasses. . . ."

"Just like *Kevin's*?" I asked her teasingly. Kate grinned. I could tell she'd changed her mind about a certain actor.

"What should we do now?" Patti asked.

"Let's watch some TV," Stephanie suggested, flopping down on the bed.

"What's on tonight?" I wondered.

Patti checked the listings. "A science-fiction double-feature . . . and two hours of reruns of *Made for Each Other!*" she exclaimed.

Before, Kate would have groaned at the thought of even half an hour of Kevin. But not this time. "What channel?" she said, switching on the little portable on Patti's desk. Then she slipped on her glasses.

Stephanie raised her eyebrow at Kate. "I think Kevin DeSpain has a new fan!" she murmured.

And for the rest of the evening, at least, the Sleepover Friends were in absolute, total agreement!

#21, STARSTRUCK STEPHANIE

The late bell rang, and math class began. Ms. Chipley opened Mrs. Mead's gradebook and picked the names of four kids to work out some of the homework problems on the blackboard. Patti was one of the kids she called on.

Patti strolled slowly up to the board, carefully picked up a piece of chalk, and proceeded to do the problem *wrong*! I couldn't believe it, and neither could anybody else in the room.

In science Patti couldn't seem to remember the simplest facts about circulation, like whether the veins pump blood *to* or *from* the heart. It was incredible!

By the time the lunch hour rang, Ms. Chipley was definitely starting to look worried.

WIN GIRL TALK DATE LINE –
AN AUDIO DATING GAME!

Enter the
SLEEPOVER™
FRIENDS
Date Line Giveaway!

100 Winners!

It's new! It's exciting! And you can win one! It's GIRL TALK DATE LINE ™ — the game of make-believe and fun! Play it at your next sleepover! Listen to the recorded phone calls and match up boys and girls for dates! Just fill in the coupon below and return by March 1, 1990.

Rules: Entries must be postmarked by March 1, 1990. Winners will be picked at random and notified by mail. No purchase necessary. Valid only in the U.S.A. Void where prohibited. Taxes on prizes are the responsibility of the winners and their families. Employees of Scholastic Inc.; its agencies, affiliates, subsidiaries; and their immediate families not eligible. For a complete list of winners, send a stamped, self-addressed envelope to Sleepover Friends Date Line Giveaway, Contest Winners List, at the address provided below.

Fill in the coupon below or write the information on a 3" x 5" piece of paper and mail to:
SLEEPOVER FRIENDS DATE LINE GIVEAWAY,
Scholastic Inc., P.O. Box 673, Cooper Station, New York, NY 10276.

- -

SLEEPOVER FRIENDS Date Line Giveaway

Name _____ Age _____

Street _____

City _____ State _____ Zip ____

Where did you buy this Sleepover Friends book?
☐ Bookstore ☐ Drug Store ☐ Supermarket ☐ Discount Store
☐ Book Club ☐ Book Fair ☐ Other (specify) _____

SLE689

Pack your bags for fun and adventure with

SLEEPOVER FRIENDS™

by Susan Saunders

Join Kate, Lauren, Stephanie and Patti at their great sleepover parties every weekend. Truth or Dare, scary movies, late-night boy talk–it's all part of **Sleepover Friends!**